GOODNIGHT COOPERSTOWN

by Mike Vivalo
Pictures by Jonathan Bartlett

AuthorHouse™
1663 Liberty Drive
Bloomington, IN 47403
www.authorhouse.com
Phone: 833-262-8899

Because of the dynamic nature of the Internet, any web addresses or links contained in this book may have changed since publication and may no longer be valid. The views expressed in this work are solely those of the author and do not necessarily reflect the views of the publisher, and the publisher hereby disclaims any responsibility for them.

Any people depicted in stock imagery provided by Getty Images are models, and such images are being used for illustrative purposes only.
Certain stock imagery © Getty Images.

This book is printed on acid-free paper.

ISBN: 978-1-6655-6946-0 (sc)
ISBN: 978-1-6655-6947-7 (e)

Print information available on the last page.

Published by AuthorHouse 09/20/2022

authorHOUSE®

GOODNIGHT COOPERSTOWN

By Mike Vivalo

Pictures by Jonathan Bartlett

In Cooperstown New York
There is a building
Full of baseball's best
And a picture of...

Willie Mays making a basket catch

**There's Joltin' Joe
who hit in 56 games in a row**

And Ty Cobb and Mel Ott
and Babe Ruth calling his shot

And Cal Ripken's steak

And Lou Gehrig's speech

And Winfield and Mo

And Jeter's jump throw

And Seaver and Gwynn

And Number 42   **Jackie Robinson**

And plaques on the walls telling stories of all

Goodnight
baseball's best

Goodnight Willie Mays making a basket catch

Goodnight Joltin' Joe
Goodnight 56 games in a row

Goodnight Ty Cobb and Mel Ott
Goodnight Babe Ruth calling his shot

Goodnight Nolan Ryan the Strikeout King

Goodnight Ken Griffey Jr's beautiful swing

Goodnight Kirby Puckett and Mike Schmidt

Yogi, Scooter and The Mick

Goodnight Hammerin' Hank

Goodnight Ernie Banks

Goodnight Cy Young
Goodnight Bob Gibson

And Goodnight Greg Maddux,
John Smoltz and Tom Glavine

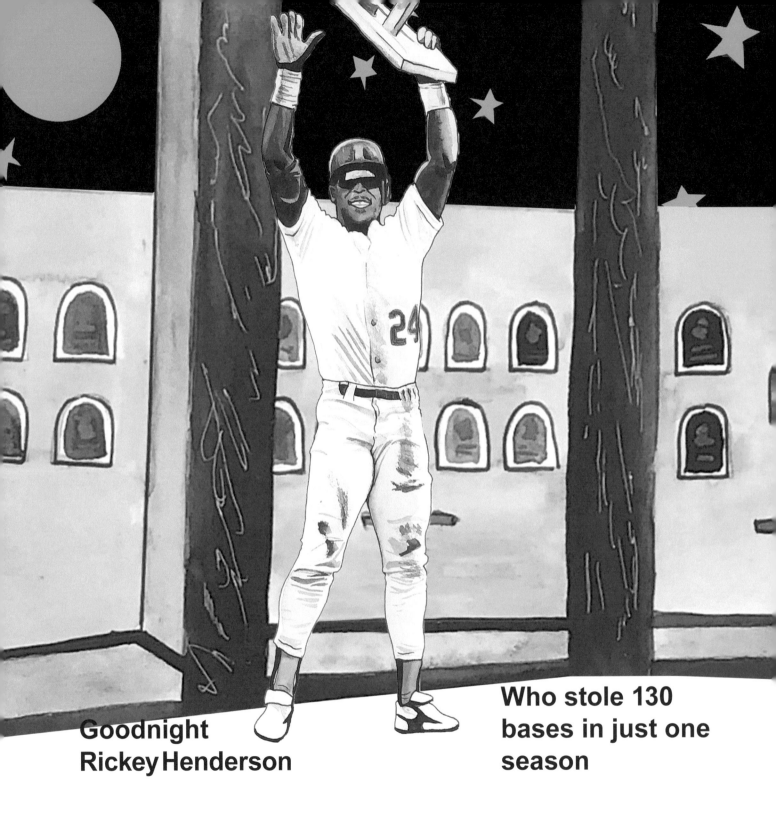

Goodnight
Rickey Henderson

Who stole 130
bases in just one
season

Goodnight Sandy Koufax

Goodnight Mr. October

**And Goodnight Ted Williams,
the Splendid Splinter**

Goodnight Ozzie's back flip
Goodnight Fisk waving fair

**Goodnight Baseball
Legends Everywhere**

Printed in the United States
by Baker & Taylor Publisher Services